MONSTER MANNERS

by JOANNA COLE

pictures by JARED LEE

SCHOLASTIC INC.
New York Toronto London Auckland Sydney

Reading level is determined by using
the Spache Readability Formula.
2.0 signifies low second grade level.

ISBN 0-590-40926-3

Text copyright © 1985 by Joanne Cole
Illustrations copyright © 1985 by Jared Lee
All rights reserved. Published by Scholastic Inc.

12 11 10 9 8 7   6 7 8 9/9

Printed in the U.S.A.   40

To Rachel

Rosie Monster looked like
a perfect little monster.
She had nice strong teeth,
and sharp little claws,
and green eyes that
glowed in the dark.

Rosie had just one problem.
She was always forgetting
her monster manners.

Monsters are supposed
to fight with their friends
and break each other's toys.

Rosie played nicely with everyone.

This made her mother very unhappy.

Monsters are supposed
to growl loudly
when they answer the telephone.

Rosie always forgot
and said "Hello"
in a polite voice.

Her father found this very upsetting.

Monsters are supposed
to chew up rocks
to show how fierce they are.

After one bite,
Rosie would stop crunching
and run for her toothbrush.
She didn't like the way
the bits of rock got stuck
between her teeth.

One day, when the family
was out walking,
Rosie even helped an old man
cross the street.

Her mother and father
shook their heads.
"I'm afraid Rosie will
never learn," said her father.
"How will she get along
in the world?" asked her mother.

While they were talking,
Rosie's best friend, Prunella, came by.

"You have good manners, Prunella,"
said Rosie. "Will you teach me?"

"Sure," said Prunella.

And so Prunella came over
to give Rosie some lessons.

The first lesson was making
monster faces.

Prunella showed Rosie
how to make

Monster Face Number
One . . .

Monster Face Number
Two . . .

Monster Face Number
Three . . .

and Monster Face Number
Four.

Then it was Rosie's turn.
She tried Monster Face Number One,

then Number Two... Number Three...

and Number Four.

"That's terrible," said Prunella.
"Let's try something else.
     Maybe you're better at table manners."

Prunella took Rosie
to a restaurant
and ordered lunch.

Everyone fainted when
Prunella started to eat.
What a horrible sight!

Rosie forgot
her monster manners,
as usual.
She used her napkin,
and her fork and spoon.
And when she asked
Prunella to pass the salt,
she forgot again
and said "Please."

Prunella was angry.
"You're not even trying,"
she said.

Prunella decided to give Rosie
one more chance.

"This time we will practice our
visiting manners," she said.

"We'll drop in on my Uncle Ned."

Prunella behaved perfectly
for a monster.
First she rang the door bell
ten times without stopping —
even when she heard her uncle say,
"Come in."

Then Prunella knocked so hard
the door fell down.
She went inside
and jumped up and down
on her uncle's favorite chair.

She spilled a vase
of flowers on the rug.

And finally she stepped
very hard
on Uncle Ned's foot.
Uncle Ned was
proud of Prunella.

But Rosie said,
"How do you do?"
and sat quietly on the sofa.
Uncle Ned was horrified.
He asked Prunella
to take her friend home
until she could learn
better manners.

Prunella threw up her hands.
"I did my best, Rosie,"
she said.
"I can't do any more."

Rosie hung her head
and followed Prunella.
For the first time,
Rosie realized how unhappy
she had made everyone.
And now she felt unhappy, too.

When Rosie and Prunella
got to the Monsters' house,
they saw a big mess.
A pipe had broken
and water was pouring
everywhere.

"Help!" cried Rosie.
"We're getting flooded."
Rosie's mother and father
came running.

Rosie's mother called the plumber
and growled into the phone.
The plumber hung up.

Rosie's father called and
roared into the phone.
The plumber hung up harder.

Prunella tried, too,
but the same thing happened.

They were getting nowhere,
and the water was getting deeper.

Something had to be done.
And Rosie did it.
Without thinking,
she dialed the phone
and said in a nice voice,
"Hello. We have a leak
at the Monsters' house.
Can you come over, please?"

"I'll be right there,"
said the plumber.
"Thank you," said Rosie.

After the plumber had left
and everything was back
to normal,
Rosie's mother turned
to Rosie's father.

"You know, dear," she said,
"Rosie's strange manners
do come in handy sometimes."

"We're lucky to have her,"
said Rosie's father,
"strange manners and all."

They gave Rosie
a hug and a kiss
and sent her out to play.

"Mind your manners, dear,"
called Rosie's mother
from the window.

"I will, Mother,"
answered Rosie.

About the Author

Joanna Cole has written more than twenty books for children. She especially likes to write about science. Two of her other books published by Scholastic are BONY-LEGS and DINOSAUR STORY. She lives in New York City with her husband, her daughter, two dogs, and no cats.

About the Artist

Jared Lee has illustrated over a dozen books, half of them for children. He has also designed posters for the U.S. Postal Service and McDonalds Restaurants. Mr. Lee lives in Lebanon, Ohio.